W9-CHX-073

Copyright © 1988 by Greey de Pencier Books. Published in the U.S.A. by Grosset &
Dunlap, Inc., a member of The Putnam Publishing Group. All rights reserved. Printed
in Hong Kong. Library of Congress Catalog Number: 87-81716
ISBN 0-448-09276-X   B C D E F G H I J

Simultaneously published in Canada by Greey de Pencier Books under the title
I DIDN'T KNOW THAT!

*OWL is a trademark of The Young Naturalist Foundation. No part of this book may
be reproduced or copied in any form without written permission from the publishers.

Editors: Sylvia Funston   Art Direction: Wycliffe Smith
          Katherine Farris   Cover Photo: Tony Thomas

THE KIDS'
Question&Answer
BOOK TWO

From the editors of OWL Magazine

GROSSET & DUNLAP · NEW YORK
A member of The Putnam Publishing Group

Did you ever wonder

why you wake up every morning? Or why certain things happen every day? Did you ever have a question about something really ordinary that *nobody* could answer? If so, this book's for you. It gives you the answers to some of your most baffling everyday questions . . . and to lots more you never even thought to wonder about.

Did *you know, for example, that you'll drink at least the equivalent of 40,000 glasses full of liquid in your lifetime? Or that almost every part of your body contains water – even your bones? So much for "bone dry." Speaking of bones, did you know your hands contain more than one-quarter of all the bones in your body? And that there's no such thing as being double-jointed? You might be able to amaze people by bending your thumbs to your wrists, but that's because you have lazy or loose joints. Some people are born this way: their joints are missing protective bands of tissue called ligaments. Other people damage their ligaments by over-stretching them. So thumb benders beware!*

"All this talk of bending and stretching brings us to the subject of exercise. Did you know that, unlike an elephant whose heart only beats forty times per minute, the average heart rate for a 10-year-old, *at rest*, is around 85 beats per minute? This gives a staggering total of 122,400 beats in a single day – and that's before you do any heart accelerating exercise. Imagine what happens to your heart rate after you've been running around in gym class for thirty minutes!

If you want a real workout, try push-ups. But next time you've got your nose to the carpet take a good look. Ever wonder where all that dust comes from? Dust is made up of flakes of skin, pavement grit, tiny live insects called dust mites, weensy insect skeletons, ash, salt from the sea, sand, the eggs of fleas, and microscopic shreds of clothing – just to name a few of the bits and pieces. And get this. The earth weighs 5,974,000,000,000,000,000,000 tons, and part of its weight problem comes from the fact that it gains 10 tons *a day* from space dust. That's enough to make anyone sneeze. By the way, did you know that a sneeze travels at 160 km/h/100 mph? That's as fast as a hurricane-force wind.

As long as a hurricane isn't blowing, why not step outside and into the sun? Did you know it takes eight minutes for sunlight to travel from the sun to Earth? Perhaps you'll feel like going for a walk. Did you know the average person walks more than 11 million km/6.9 million miles in their lifetime? If you do go for a walk, you might find the streets more crowded than ever. After all, 152 babies are born every minute. And the United Nations estimated that at the end of June 1987 the world's five-billionth baby was born. Chances are that at least one of the people you'll pass on your walk will be having a birthday. Why? Thirteen million people have a birthday today.

While you're trying to nudge past all those crowds of people, look down. You'll probably see a crowd of ants swarming around a crack in the sidewalk. Why? They're either foraging for food that people have dropped or they're leaving or entering their nest. Not many species of ants nest underneath the concrete slabs, but those that do have found themselves a good home. The concrete absorbs the warmth of the sun during the day and radiates it back during the evening. So the ants keep warm both day and night.

After all this messing around in the dirt, it's probably time for a bath. Would it surprise you to know that there is enough water in the world's oceans to fill 6,439,910,400,000,000,000 bathtubs? Once bathed and clean, it's time for bed. But before you doze off, did you know that when at night you go to sleep you've just lived through 23 hours, 56 minutes and 4.09 seconds of another day? And just think, tomorrow there will be something new to wonder about. Turn the page to find out more.

Why do you wake up?

It's the weekend and you don't need to get up early. So why do you wake up on a sleep-in Saturday the same time you wake up on school days? Your internal "alarm clock" tells you it's time to wake up. But what sets your "alarm clock" to go off? Sunlight does. If you lived totally in the dark your internal clock would run slower and slower until you ended up sleeping and waking at very odd times. But sunlight resets your clock every day, so you operate on a more-or-less 24-hour schedule – just like the planet you live on.

Why does sunshine make you feel good?

When you wake up on a sunny day, getting up seems easy. Why? Sunlight, especially early morning light, helps to keep your body's biological rhythm in line. And when your body's rhythm is "in beat," you feel good. Most people aren't really aware how much they need sunlight until they get the short dark days of fall and winter. Then the lack of sunlight can be a real problem for some people. It causes their biological rhythm to go haywire and they become sleepy, cranky and sad. But scientists have found that exposing these people daily to bright light helps to keep them alert and happy.

Why does my cat pat me with its paw every morning?

Touch is an important way for cats to show affection. If your cat touches your face with its paw it's saying, "You're a member of my family." If it rubs against your legs, it's leaving a scent on you that marks you as a close companion. And occasionally your cat may even touch you nose to nose. Touch your cat's nose with yours once in a while to kiss back.

Why do butterflies lie on my lawn in the morning?

Butterflies don't lie around in the morning because they're lazy. They have a different problem: dew droplets on their wings weigh them down and make flying impossible. That's why, before they can take off, dew-drenched butterflies must sunbathe until the sun's heat has dried them off.

Why does thick syrup pile up when it's poured?

When you pour milk over shredded wheat, it flows evenly over the cereal. But when you pour thick syrup onto pancakes, the syrup piles up on itself. Why? Syrup's thick, sticky consistency causes it to hold together. So when it's poured, the bottom part of the drip touches the surface of the syrup but doesn't disappear into the body of the syrup. Instead it folds over, piling up into little mounds. But after a moment those little mounds flatten out and the thick, sticky syrup cascades down the sides of your pancakes. Yum.

Why does it hurt if you bite on tinfoil?

That sharp pain you feel is actually a weak electric shock. Where does the electricity come from? If you've got a filling and bite on another kind of metal such as tinfoil, your slightly acid saliva turns your mouth into an electricity-producing battery. The electric current passes through your saliva between the filling and the foil. Unfortunately it keeps going right through the filling into the sensitive nerve of your tooth. Then – zap! Ouch!

Why do most cereals crackle when you add milk to them?

When milk sits in a carton in the fridge, it's perfectly quiet. And when rice cereal sits in its box, it doesn't crackle or pop. So why all the noise when you mix the two together? It has to do with the way the cereal is made. Rice cereal is made by heating the ingredients at very high temperatures. When that happens, water inside each bit of rice expands suddenly and blows it up like a balloon, leaving each piece with very tiny cavities all over its surface. (If you look closely at your cereal, or put a piece under a magnifying glass, you'll see these tiny holes.) When milk is added, it flows over these little cavities and traps air inside them. Then, as the milk slowly starts to seep into the tiny holes, it forces the air out. And it's that air being released that you hear as a "pop" or a "crackle."

Why do people get thirsty?

If you feel thirsty it's because you've lost more water than you've taken in. How do you lose water? By sweating and by elimination. Your body needs lots of water and it will let you know if you should drink up. How? Thirst receptors in the back of your throat dry up and make you feel parched. When this happens your brain sends out the message, "Hey, drink up!"

Salty foods can also make you feel thirsty. Why? Salt absorbs water. When you cram a handful of chips into your mouth, the salt on them dries out your thirst receptors, leaving you with that familiar dry-mouthed feeling. Once you've taken a drink of something you'll feel better. That is, of course, until you cram in the next handful of chips.

Why do table knives have round ends?

The knife was one of our earliest inventions, used for fighting, hunting, carving and, of course, for cutting food. The problem of people fighting with knives at mealtimes brought about the invention of table manners. In 1699, the king of France ruled that table knives should have round ends to stop dinner guests from sticking knives into each other or picking their teeth with the cutlery. Table knives have had round ends ever since.

Who first used forks?

Rich people were the first to use forks, to keep their lace-ruffled sleeves out of the gravy. As the custom spread, the way food was served changed too. Instead of everyone taking food from a shared dish, each diner got an individual helping. The invention of the fork also ended the need for washing our hands during dinner: a table napkin is all we need.

Why don't bananas have seeds?

Unzip a banana and take a look at what's inside. Lots of sweet pulp and no seeds means that the banana doesn't grow naturally in the wild – it's an "invention" of ours. Thousands of years ago, wild bananas looked like big bean pods filled with seeds. It wasn't until Southeast Asians learned how to breed pulpy, seedless bananas that bananas started to look as they do today. Some bananas are not sweet. They are picked green and boiled, made into beer, fried, broiled, dried or turned into soup. Only sweet bananas are eaten raw. And here in North America, more sweet bananas are eaten every day than any other fruit.

Why do bananas get bruised as they age?

Bananas turn black as they get older even if they've never been touched, so those black spots aren't bruises. They're caused by a hormone called ethylene that helps fruit ripen. Unfortunately, ethylene doesn't know when to stop ripening, and eventually it turns the banana black. There's no way to prevent the production of ethylene, although you can slow it down by storing your bananas in a cool place. But keep them out of the refrigerator or you'll have the spottiest bananas on the block before you can say "peanut butter and banana sandwich."

What makes your stomach growl?

Next time you're sitting in a quiet classroom just before lunch, listen for the sound of growling stomachs. Doctors call this "borborygmi," which sounds a bit like the noise you hear. It happens when your stomach walls automatically squeeze together in an attempt to mix and digest food and there's no food there. Gases and digestive juices slosh around inside your empty stomach and before you know it . . . borborygmi, borborygmi.

BORBORYGMI!

Why are there holes in Swiss cheese?

It has to do with "burping" bacteria. Here's how. Cheese is made by adding bacteria to milk. Swiss cheese is made with a special type of long-acting bacteria. These bacteria gobble up milk sugars and burp out gas long after the cheese has been covered with rind. And because the rind is airtight, the gas gathers in pockets in the cheese causing holes.

13

Why do apples turn brown after you cut into them?

When you cut through the skin of an apple, you expose its white flesh to the air. When that happens, naturally occuring phenolic compounds in the apple oxidize – mix with oxygen in the air and cause the exposed flesh to turn brown. This browning is the apple's natural defense mechanism. It stops the oxidization from destroying the rest of the apple, at least for a while. You can slow down the browning by soaking the apple in lemon juice. That stops the air from getting at the apple.

Why do jumping beans jump?

Jumping beans jump because there's something alive inside. A jumping bean is actually the seed of a Mexican shrub. Inside the seed is the larva of a tiny moth. When the seeds are left in a warm place, the larva starts to move around. And that causes the jumping bean to tumble and jump.

What's the oldest vegetable on earth?

t's hard to pin down the oldest vegetable on earth, but we do know that by 6000 BC people in the Near East were eating lentils. Scientists also believe that, halfway around the world, beans, peas, gourds and water chestnuts were being cultivated in the Far East, and that people living in what is now Mexico were growing gourds, beans and pumpkins. So when you start carving out faces next Halloween just think, pumpkins are almost 8,000 years old!

What kind of shells do cashews come in?

Before we get into a cashew's shell we should first tell you that a cashew isn't really a nut . . .it's a seed that grows on a tropical evergreen tree in Central and South America. Cashews are quite extraordinary.

They grow out of the end of a pear-shaped fruit called the cashew apple which is about three times as large as a cashew and is used to make jam. The cashew doesn't have a hard, leathery, "nutty" shell. Instead it's protected by two layers of casing. Cashews are related to mangoes and poison ivy. Raw cashews are poisonous. But roasting destroys the poison.

Is a tomato a fruit or a vegetable?

A tomato is a fruit. And if you want to be specific you can rightfully call it a "berry." It grows on a plant that's part of the nightshade family, so its cousins are eggplants, potatoes and tobacco. When tomatoes were first introduced into Europe people wouldn't eat them, because they thought they were poisonous.

Why do apples crunch?

Apples – and, for that matter, lettuce, celery and carrots – crunch because they're composed of cells that are filled with water. When you chomp into an apple, these cells explode and tiny spurts of water burst out. Those little explosions make that satisfying CRUNCH. How loud the crunch is depends on how strong the cell walls are. If the walls are strong and can take a lot of pressure (like those of an apple), the crunch is good and loud. If they're weak (like those of an orange), there's no real crunch at all.

How much water is in a watermelon?

Watermelons are perfectly named. They're 93% water. In a really big 45 kg/100 lb watermelon, the amount of water inside could weigh more than you!

Why are flowers different colors?

Today we breed flowers in a whole rainbow of colors. But in the wild, flowers grow in different colors to attract certain birds and insects to help pollinate them. If a flower wants a bee pollinator, for instance, it will have better luck if it is yellow or blue. Those are the colors bees prefer. Moths like pale-colored flowers, while birds and butterflies are attracted to bright colors. Why are there so few green flowers in the wild? It seems that not many birds or insects like the color green.

How does a sprouting seed know which way is up?

Seeds respond to gravity just like you do. How? Little granules in the growing tips react to gravity and help orient the seedlings' growth. That's why no matter which way a seed is planted, it always manages to snake its root and shoot around so that the root grows down and the shoot grows up. Plants depend on gravity for their directions so much that when they're put into zero-gravity tanks, they get confused and grow any which way. This means that space gardeners will have to grow their plants in artificial gravity or be prepared to teach them which way is up.

How much paper does one tree make?

You could make a stack of newspapers about 1.3 m/4 feet tall from one average-sized tree. Does that seem like a lot of news to you? Well, here's some more news: the most massive living thing in the world is still alive and well in California . . .and it's a giant sequoia tree. More than 20 children holding hands could barely manage to circle it. And not only that, but there's enough wood in one giant sequoia to make 50 average-sized houses.

Which tree has the longest roots?

It depends on the kind of roots. Some trees have a long, tapered "tap" root that looks like an underground trunk. The longest tap root ever found belonged to an enormous fig tree in South Africa and went straight down 133 m/400 feet. Other trees, such as the oak, have surface roots that fan out underground in the same shape as the branches you see above ground. So the next time you're lying under a tree, looking up at the sky, just imagine how many roots you're lying on.

Do plants react when you talk to them?

Yes, but not because they find what you say particularly interesting. Plants have no sound receptors or nervous systems, so they can't hear you or detect the vibrations your voice makes. But when you talk you produce two things that plants really do react to. You breathe out carbon dioxide and water – two of the major necessities of life for all plants. So to keep your plant healthy, give it light, water and TLC (that's tender, loving chat).

Do all flowers open in the morning?

For most living things, light is like an alarm clock. It tells us when to wake up and when to go to bed. Like people, most flowers "awaken" and open their petals during the daylight. That way bees and other daytime creatures can help spread their pollen. But some flowers, such as the evening primrose, are night owls. They stay closed all day and only "wake up" at night.

How much water does a tree raise from its roots to its leaves in a day?

The giant oak can raise seven bathtubs full of water per day!

Why don't dogs' noses freeze outside in winter? ▶

The secret to a dog's frost-resistant nose lies beneath its skin: a network of tiny, hard-working blood vessels. More warm blood gets pumped here than anywhere else in the dog's body. So even though a dog's nose is wet, it never gets cold enough to freeze because of the non-stop warmth beneath its skin.

How do snakes move?

To move in a straight line, snakes use their belly scales, called "scutes," to grip the ground, a bit like treads on snow tires. Then, by shortening muscles attached to the scutes, they can pull themselves forward *inside* their skin. As soon as their belly scales release their grip, the skin moves forward too. This straight-line movement is called "creeping." Snakes can also move in S-bends, by twisting their backbones as they push off soil, sand or plant stems.

How can mice squeeze themselves into such small spaces?

Chances are you've watched in astonishment as a tiny mouse suddenly darted across the floor and disappeared into a hole so small you didn't even know it was there. Mice and rats have to be able to quickly squeeze into hiding places too small for their enemies. Both mice and rats have torpedo-shaped bodies, topped by sharp, pointed heads. This makes them well streamlined for sliding in and out of tight spaces, and their soft, glossy fur and flexible joints help them slip past obstacles.

18

Why does my goldfish hit the sides of its bowl?

Bump! Your goldfish can't easily distinguish between the glass and the water, so it has to use its sense of touch. Also, the edge of the bowl and the water may create an optical illusion that makes it difficult for your goldfish to tell the difference between the two. Dark paper taped to an outer wall may help your pet locate this side less painfully.

Why does my budgie fly into the wall when I let it out of the cage?

Your budgie doesn't have much room in a cage to master the difficult art of flying. It has to learn how to turn, bank, ride air currents and do many other things it can't practice in a small space. And since it's not used to wide open spaces it may have problems judging distance. But if you can let your budgie out of its cage more often, you'll quickly see it develop into a flying ace.

Why doesn't it hurt a kitten when its mother picks it up by the neck?

All cats have very sharp teeth, but the mother cat knows just how firmly she can pick up her kitten so that she won't bite into its skin. She also is careful to pick it up by the furry "handle" of loose skin around the kitten's neck. Because the kitten is so light, there's not much weight pulling down on this handle. Also, almost all cats instinctively stop moving when they're picked up by the loose skin around the neck.

Do pets watch TV?

It's unlikely your cat will become a rock video fan or your dog will turn into a soap opera addict, but animals do watch TV. Even though they see little or no color, cats and dogs are attracted to the movement they see on TV, probably because of their hunting instincts. Perhaps the action reminds them of small scurrying animals. But the main reason they watch TV is to keep you company. Most pets also like music and some even join in and "sing" along.

How do dogs smell so well?

Animals depend on their sense of smell much more than you do, and their noses show it. For instance, in each nostril you have barely enough smell cells to cover a small stamp. But in a dog's nose the smelling area is more than five times that big and packed with 20 times as many smell cells. Bloodhounds have such a keen sense of smell they can follow a trail several hours old.

Why do horses have "scabs" on their legs?

Those scab-like patches high on the insides of horses' legs are known as "chestnuts," and they're what's left of thumbs horses once had. The first horse ancestor was the size of a dog and had four toes per foot. Gradually, three of these toes fused into a hoof, which meant the horse could run faster. Once it had hooves, its thumbs – the fourth toes – were useless and slowly vanished, leaving only the chestnuts. They're high on the legs because as horses evolved their foot bones grew longer. How much longer? Take a look at your hand. A horse's front hoof is the same as the tip of your middle finger, its ankle compares to the knuckle at the base of that finger and its knee is the same as your wrist.

What's the difference between hair and fur?

In a sense there's no difference. Fur is made of densely packed hair – so fur is hair . . . and so are whiskers and quills. Some animals have two types of fur. They have a thick coat of short, fine hairs that insulates the body and an overcoat of long guard hairs that sheds water.

What's the hairiest animal alive? The musk ox wins hooves down. Its 1 m/ 3 foot-long hair keeps it warm no matter how cold the weather gets.

Why don't dogs' nails grow?

You might think that your dog's nails never grow, but the fact is they do! And some dogs' nails grow so long that they have to be taken to the vet to have them clipped. But really all a dog needs to keep its nails trim is a sidewalk. Walking on cement is like walking on nature's nail file.

Why do spiders spin webs?

Spiders spin webs to trap insects to eat. The webs are made of silk that the spider manufactures in special silk glands in its abdomen. The webs most often found in houses are cobwebs. But in gardens you're likely to see orb webs. They look like bicycle wheels with radiating spokes. Although spider webs are strong enough to catch insects, they do get damaged. To repair a damaged web, spiders eat up the wrecked bits and spin new silk to repair the holes. If the damage is really bad, they'll eat up all the remaining bits and spin an entirely new web. Not all spiders spin a traditional web to trap insects. These four spiders, for example, have developed other ingenious ways to catch their lunch.

The ogre-faced spider hangs upside-down holding a bug-catching net between its front legs. When an insect passes by, the ogre stretches open its net and sweeps it down over its victim.

H yptiotes spins its triangular web, then holds on to one corner thread. When an insect flies into the web, Hyptiotes lets its thread go slack so that the web collapses around the insect in a tangled mess.

T he bola spider sits quietly waiting for a tasty insect to fly by. When a victim comes near, the bola throws a ball of glue attached to a silken line. If its aim is good, its dinner sticks to the glue ball, and all the bola has to do is reel in dinner.

Moths escape from most webs by shedding their wing scales. To trap them, the ladder web spider builds a long, escape-proof web. When a moth flies into this "ladder," it flip-flops down to the bottom, losing all its scales. Then it's stuck for good.

Why do roosters crow in the morning?

Long ago when chickens were wild, roosters crowed so loudly to attract a mate that they were in danger of being pounced on by a predator looking for a chicken dinner. To avoid being seen, they began to do most of their crowing when the light was dim – in the early morning and late afternoon. Today's equally loud-mouthed roosters still crow most at those two times. But early in the morning you notice them more because there's usually not a lot of other noises going on then to distract you.

Why do dogs circle around before they lie down?

Your dog circles around to prepare a safe and comfortable "nest" for itself to sleep in. Sound strange? It's an old habit, practiced by wild dogs who circled around to make sure no predators were lurking and to trample down the grass to make their nest more comfy. Dogs aren't the only animals that have this kind of "nesting behavior." For example, some people plump up their pillows before they crawl into bed. What special way do you have of making your "nest" cozy too?

Why are cats so difficult to teach?

Cats aren't stupid. It's just that they've never learned to take orders like dogs have. Your dog's wild relatives lived in packs that were run by a pack leader. Your dog thinks of you as his pack leader, and instinctively wants to obey and please you. But your cat's wild relatives lived on their own and didn't take orders from anyone. And neither does your tabby.

How do worms see underground?

Worms don't have eyes like we do, so they have to feel their way around. Fortunately they move so slowly that they don't hurt themselves if they bump into something. At the surface, worms use light-sensitive organs on their heads and tails to detect harsh, bright sunlight that might dry them out. When they sense bright lights, they retreat back underground to the safety of darkness.

Why do fish lay so many eggs?

Because most fish lay their eggs in the open and don't stay around to protect them, they produce thousands of eggs, gambling that at least a few will survive. On the other hand, some fish don't need to lay so many eggs because they put them in safe places. Sticklebacks, for instance, make "nests" for their eggs, while female sea horses deposit their eggs in a special brood pouch on the male sea horse's belly.

Why do ▶ monkeys groom each other?

When someone shakes your hand, hugs you or even pats you on the back, they're trying to tell you something – that you're part of a group. Touching acts as "social glue" and helps keep groups together. Monkeys don't shake hands, but they do spend several hours a day grooming each other. This not only keeps them clean; it also helps to keep them together as a group, just as physical contact does among people.

Why does a rabbit wiggle its nose?

By wiggling its nose a rabbit can test air from many directions at once. This gives the rabbit a better chance of sniffing out any hidden enemies. But nose wiggling's not as easy as it looks. In fact, a rabbit is one of the few animals that has enough control over the nerves and muscles in its nose to be able to twitch the tip of it. Even though pet rabbits don't have to worry about enemies nearly as much as wild rabbits do, they still wiggle their noses; perhaps it lets them know when their owner is bringing them a treat.

Why do flies walk all over your food?

Flies don't walk all over your food just for the exercise. They do it so they can taste what they're about to eat. How? The tiny hairs on their feet act like the tastebuds on your tongue.

Why does a wood-pecker hammer on trees? Does it hurt? ▶

A woodpecker hammers on trees to get at its lunch. How does it know where to drill? It listens. Clinging to the bark, the woodpecker listens for bark beetles or larvae boring holes in the tree. When it hears them, the woodpecker starts drilling. Once it gets close to its dinner the woodpecker extends its long tongue into the hole and pulls out the food.

All that hammering doesn't hurt the wood-pecker, because it's well built to withstand such action. It has a very thick skull, extra-large muscles in its neck and around its skull, and a very stiff tail, all of which help to absorb and cushion the blows.

Why does my dog stretch whenever I come in?

When your dog meets you at the door in this posture, it's not stretching, it's saying, "Hello, glad to see you." At any other time this posture means "Please play with me." If you want to play, get down on your knees, stretch out your arms and let your dog know.

Why does my cat yawn all the time?

If your cat yawns around you, don't be insulted. All it's saying is, "I'm relaxed around you." Yawn back or blink slowly and you'll give your cat the same message.

Why do chickens peck each other?

How is a group of chickens like a large corporation? They both have "pecking orders" that keep the group organized and running smoothly. In a big corporation, there's usually a boss, a second in command and so on down the line. Chickens use the same system, but in their case there's a lot of real pecking involved. Here's how it works. The "boss" chicken can peck all the birds below it. Bird number 2 can peck all but the boss. Bird number 3 can peck all but the boss and number 2, and so on down the line. All that pecking keeps even the most rebellious chicken in line.

Why does it hurt when you laugh really hard?

When someone tells you a joke and you start to laugh really hard, you tense up your stomach muscles and pump your diaphragm up and down. If you keep on laughing you end up with over-exercised stomach and diaphragm muscles – and they hurt! But just think.

Some people get the same kind of soreness by doing push-ups. At least it's more fun to laugh.

Why does laughing make you feel good?

Believe it or not, laughter is basically a tension release mechanism. When your body feels tense, it seeks a way to get rid of its tension. Exercise is one way, but laughter is equally effective. And once the tension is gone you feel better.

Why do people burp?

People burp because they've swallowed air. Sometimes people take huge gulps of air when they eat – for instance when they swallow soup and try to cool it at the same time.

Other times, there's lots of air in what they're eating or drinking – for example, soda pop. When the carbon dioxide is released in the stomach, the air comes up, bubbles over the back of the throat and – oops, excuse me!

Why do your eyes cry when you're laughing really hard?

Take a close look at someone who's laughing really hard. Their face is all squeezed up and their mouth is probably wide open. If you took a picture and showed it to a friend, your friend probably wouldn't be able to tell if the person was laughing or yawning. Your eyes "cry" when you laugh, just as they "cry" when you yawn. Why? That squeezed-up face puts pressure on the tear glands. If the glands are full, tears will drop out.

Who first used umbrellas?

Only extremely important people were allowed to use umbrellas or parasols in ancient China, India, Persia and Africa. The King of Burma called himself The Lord of the Great Parasol. These early umbrellas were colorful, large and impressive; a crowd could easily pick out the important person with an umbrella when nobody else had one. One of the first umbrellas in Europe was brought there from Persia by Jonas Hanway in 1750. People who saw him walking with it thought he was quite mad.

Why are storm clouds gray, while other clouds are white?

Lie outside on your back on a sunny day and watch the clouds go by. Notice many all-white clouds? Probably not – even fine-weather clouds have some gray parts. That's because some part of each cloud is in shadow – and it's the shadows that cause the gray. The gray color is also caused by water droplets in the cloud – the bigger the drops, the darker the cloud. On stormy days there are lots of water droplet-filled clouds around casting shadows. When you see them, get out your umbrella.

Why do we get rosy cheeks in winter?

You can't always protect your face by bundling up, so your brain has come up with a way to protect your exposed skin from frostbite. If your cheeks get cold, your brain sends a "warm up" signal to a network of fine blood vessels under the skin. These vessels enlarge so that more warm blood can flow through them and heat up your cheeks. It's this increased blood flow just beneath the skin that gives your cheeks their rosy glow.

What does "It smells like rain" mean?

Almost everything smells stronger before it rains. Why? It has to do with the force of air pressing down on you. During fine weather the air pressure is high, but it drops before a storm. This lower pressure allows odors to escape into the air more freely than usual. So it's not the rain you're smelling – you're smelling more of everything.

What's a nose for? ■

Your nose does a lot more than just take up space between your eyes. Not only does it bring in air and let you smell and taste things; it also prepares the air for your lungs by warming it up. The hairs in your nose – the ones you can see as well as microscopic ones – filter the air and prevent particles from entering your lungs. And your nose also acts as an echo chamber to give your voice its unique sound.

Why does sniffing hard help you smell better?

If someone gave you a rose, what would be the first thing you'd do? You'd probably sniff it. Usually when you breathe, not much air moves up to the very top of your nose where your smell cells are. But when you sniff you breathe in a lot more air and you aim it right at your nose's smell center.

Why do noses run?

Your nose is always producing mucus, but sometimes it makes too much. Then it's quick, pass the tissues! When you cry your nose runs because some of your tears drip down overflow tubes that connect your eyes to your nose. Your nose also runs to flush out dirt and germs.

Why can't you taste anything when you've got a cold?

You're tired, your eyes are sore and when your nose isn't running it's all stuffed up. That's right: you've got a cold. And one of the worst things about having a cold is that your tongue feels funny and everything tastes like cardboard. Why? Because your nose is full of gooey mucus and no air can reach your smell cells. And that's where the trouble lies. Without your sense of smell you can hardly taste the difference between foul-tasting medicine and chocolate milk.

Why do eyes sometimes look red in photos?

If all your photographs turn your friends into red-eye fiends, take heart. What you've done is aimed your flash directly into their eyes. When the light flashes, you capture on film a very neat photo of the inside of everyone's eyeballs. They're red because they contain lots of blood vessels. To avoid that wild-eyed look on future photos, either tell your friends to look slightly away from the flash or, if possible, hold the flashgun off to the side and then click.

Do blind people dream?

Yes. Blind people who could once see can still "see" in their dreams. But people who have been blind from birth have dreams with no pictures. Their dreams are full of smell, taste, touch and sound sensations.

What's wrong with your eyes if you're color blind?

Being color blind only affects how you see colors, not how well you see. People with full color vision have three types of cone-shaped cells in their eyes. One type of cone sees red light, another green and the third blue. A color blind person is missing one or more types of cones. Red-green color blindness is the most common and occurs when the red or green cones are absent. People with this type of color blindness see red or green as gray-brown. Here's a test for red-green color blindness. What number do you see in this group of dots?
(Answer: If you saw the number 15, then you have normal color vision. If you saw the number 17, you may have red-green color blindness.)

Test Your Eyes

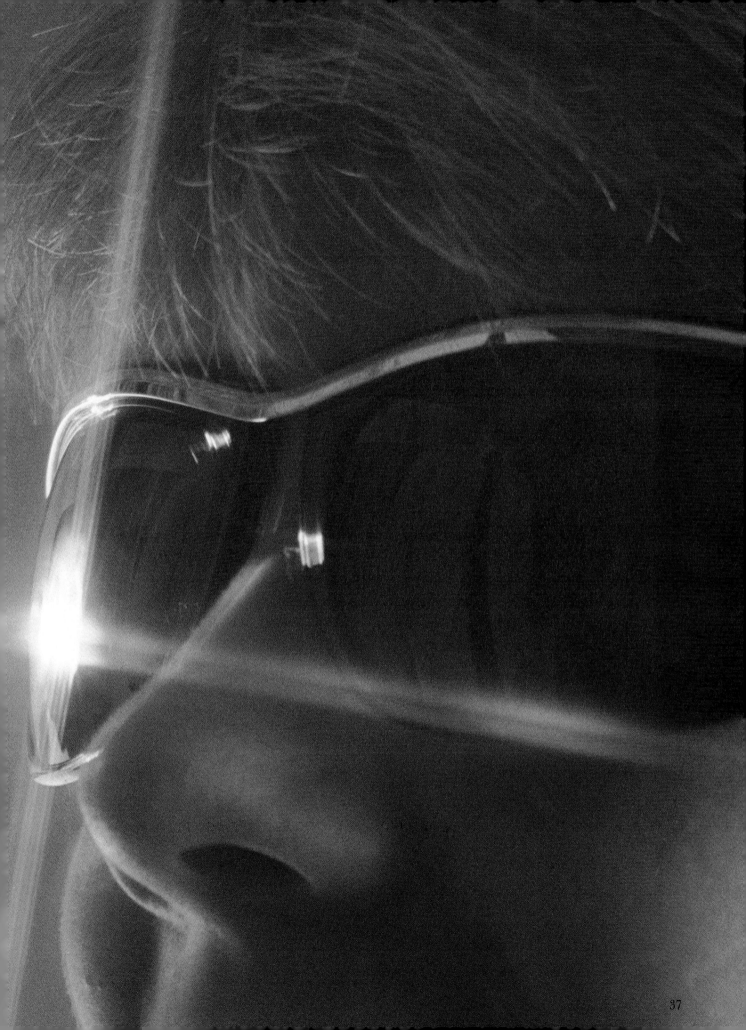

Why does your hair stand on end when you get cold or scared? ▼

When you get really scared, your nervous system sends adrenaline through your body to give you more energy. Adrenaline also makes your heart beat faster, your muscles contract and your hair stand on end. Bristly hair is especially important for an animal that's trying to scare off a predator. It makes the animal look much bigger and more ferocious. Bristly hair doesn't really help you when you're scared, but it does when it's cold. The upright hairs trap a thicker layer of air next to your skin and this insulates you better.

How does mousse keep your hair in place?

Mousse works by "gluing" your hair together. Feel your hair after moussing it and you'll know what we mean. It's the resin in mousse that makes it so sticky. (Yes, the same stuff that gives bubble gum extra stretch.) When you style a curl or wave into your hair, the resin binds the hairs together in that shape so they will all bounce back into place if they get tousled. It's almost as if the resin makes your hair remember the style you've given it. Mousse also makes your hair look thicker and fuller because it contains proteins similar to the proteins in your hair. The resin binds these proteins to your hair, making each hair shaft thicker – until you wash the mousse out.

Why does head hair grow longer than other hair?

Hairs have a natural life-span. The hairs on your head live longer than your other hairs. They grow for about two to five years before they fall out. Eyelashes, on the other hand, only last for about four months. Just imagine what would happen if your eyelashes grew as long as your hair!

How many hairs are there on a person's head?

You have about 100,000 head hairs and each one grows approximately 0.25 mm/100th of an inch a day. That may not seem like much, but if you added up the daily growth of all your hairs it would total 25 m/1,000 inches. You won't become too hairy, though, because you lose about 50 head hairs a day. That's more than 18,000 a year! Good thing they don't all fall out at once.

Why does a hot curling-iron curl your hair?

When you heat your hair with a curling-iron, you can go from straight hair to a headful of curls in just a few minutes. Why? Heat causes chains of protein molecules inside each hair to start to vibrate and pull apart. The hair then "softens" in much the same way as a sheet of plastic will soften when heated. And, like the plastic, if you shape your hair when it's soft, then let it cool, it will "harden" into the new shape. A curling-iron not only heats your hair to soften it, but it also shapes your hair into a curl.

Why do we have hair?

Millions of years ago people needed hair to keep warm. Even though you now wear clothes for warmth, you still need your hair. Eyebrows and eyelashes keep dirt out of your eyes. Head hair helps to insulate your brain from extreme temperatures. And the hair on your body acts as an early warning system to detect insects that are about to land.

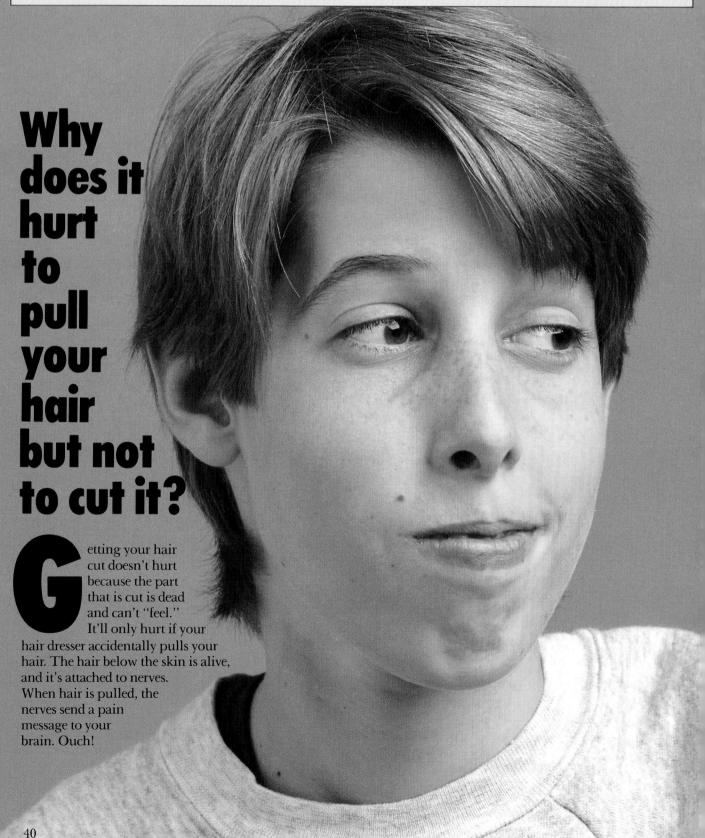

Why does it hurt to pull your hair but not to cut it?

Getting your hair cut doesn't hurt because the part that is cut is dead and can't "feel." It'll only hurt if your hair dresser accidentally pulls your hair. The hair below the skin is alive, and it's attached to nerves. When hair is pulled, the nerves send a pain message to your brain. Ouch!

Why does hair turn gray as people get older?

You may be surprised to learn that there's no such thing as gray hair. So why does your aunt look like she has gray hair, while your grandmother is crowned with a snow-white head of hair? Believe it or not, hair looks gray because pure white hairs are mixed in with colored ones. And the reason people get more white hairs as they get older is because they stop producing melanin, the substance that gives hair its color.

How can a boy tell if he'll go bald?

Nobody's really sure why people go bald, but some scientists believe that you may inherit baldness. If you're interested, check out your mother's father. Your hairline may look like his when you get older.

41

Why do you get a headache when you eat ice cream too fast? ▶

Inside your hard palate – in the roof of your mouth – is a nerve that connects with your forehead. When you eat ice cream quickly, your brain receives a message that some part of your face is getting chilled too fast for comfort. Even though it doesn't know whether it's your forehead or your hard palate that's in trouble, it responds by sending back a pain alert. And yes, you guessed it. Your forehead intercepts the message and ends up with the pain. Think of that the next time you gobble down a triple scoop chocolate fudge delight!

Does eating chocolate cause pimples?

Pimples are caused by bacteria. And these bacteria seem to thrive on oil. If you eat foods that are high in oil and fat, such as chocolate, you increase your production of oil. And more oil on your skin is just what pimple-causing bacteria enjoy. Skin specialists report that some of their patients say they break out in pimples after eating certain foods, including chocolate. But don't just blame chocolate. If you have a problem with pimples you should try to avoid any other oil producing and fat foods or foods with a high sugar content. You should also stay away from any other food that causes you problems. Other than eating a healthy diet, is there anything else you can do? If your face is greasy you should wash it two or three times a day with soap and avoid greasy make-up. Now where have you heard all that before?

Why do you itch?

An itch is a warning that there's something on your skin that shouldn't be there. This could be an insect or something you're allergic to, even sunshine. Some scientists think the itch signal travels along pain nerves to your brain, which would make an itch a mini-pain. Others think the itch signal travels along nerves reserved especially for itches. No matter how the message gets to your brain, your natural reaction is to scratch...

Does scratching stop an itch?

Nobody knows, but it certainly feels good! One theory is that scratching creates a bigger sensation, which temporarily takes your mind off the itch.

If your skin is always renewing itself, how can you have a scar for life?

The outer part of your skin, the epidermis, renews itself once every 28 days. It's made up of cells that keep pushing up towards the surface, where they die and are rubbed off by your clothing or in the shower. A scar forms when the epidermis and the layer of skin just below it are injured and replaced by scar tissue. This scar tissue is much tougher than normal and doesn't produce new cells like the surrounding tissue. That means the scar never changes and never gets rubbed off like other used-up skin cells.

The skeleton on this park bench is Bonapart, a star on OWL/TV, a children's TV show. Bonapart is *very* knowledgeable about bones. If he could talk right now, he'd be telling you that when you were born you had about 250 bones, but now you only have about 206. No, you haven't lost any. It's just that some of your bones, such as the ones in your face, have fused together. By the time you're your parents' age you'll only have about 200 bones. Read on to find out more amazing facts about your bones.

How many bones are in your head?

One, right? Wrong! The helmet of bone that protects your brain is actually seven bones that fit together like the pieces of a jigsaw puzzle.

What's the biggest bone in your body?

The biggest bone in your body is the thigh-bone or femur, the one that connects the hip-bone to the knee-bone. It's got to be big and strong to support your weight as well as all the leg muscles that are attached to it. And it's long so that you can take big strides when you're walking.

What's inside your bones?

Bones account for one-fifth of your total weight. But even though they are light-weight and can flex, they are strong enough to support you. Your bones are made up of two layers. On the outside is "compact" bone, which is thick and dense, rather like ivory. It sets the shape of the bone and anchors the muscles. The next layer is made up of "cancellous" bone, an intricate girder-like mesh. This lattice-like, honey-combed network is very light but, ounce for ounce, it is stronger than steel. Running throughout the cancellous bone are little "canals" that carry veins, arteries, cells and fluid which keep the bones strong and healthy. In the core of your bones is marrow. Marrow makes red blood cells and provides your body with an energy reserve.

What's the tiniest bone in your body?

The smallest bone in your body is in your ear. It's called the stirrup bone. Here it is. You can see how it got its name.

What keeps your bones to-gether?

Stretchy straps called ligaments tie your bones together so they don't slip out of place, but not so tight that they can't move.

Can ribs move?

The bony cage that protects your heart and lungs looks rigid but it's not. Your rib cage is loosely joined to your backbone so that the ribs can move outward. If they didn't, you wouldn't be able to breathe.

Why do my feet get cold so fast?

There's a good reason why your toes are often the first part of you to feel chilly. Heat leaves your body fastest through your toes, fingers, ears and nose. To prevent too much heat loss, your body shuts down the supply of warm blood to these areas as it tries to keep the rest of itself warm and protect sensitive organs. Without an ample supply of warm blood, your toes, fingers, ears and nose soon feel cold. In fact if it gets cold enough they'll even freeze. When that happens you've got frostbite. Ouch!

Why do feet swell up after you've been sitting for a while?

You sit down to watch a movie and slip off your shoes to get really comfortable. But when the movie's over and you try to put your shoes back on, they won't fit. Have they shrunk? No. Your feet have expanded. Because you've been sitting still, much of your body fluid has collected at your lowest point – your feet. When you get up and start walking, you'll get the fluid moving quickly again and soon your feet will shrink back to their normal size.

Why is one foot bigger than the other?

If you're like most people, one big foot isn't your only problem. You might also have mismatched arms, legs or ears. Even at birth nobody's perfect, and we sometimes become more lopsided as we grow because we use one side of our body more than the other and build up bigger muscles. These differences aren't usually a problem, but some unfortunate people have to buy two sizes of shoes to get one pair that fits!

Why do we have toes?

Without toes you probably couldn't stand up. Toes help keep you balanced, and they carry their fair share of your weight too. Your heels support half your weight, your big toes support one-quarter, and your other toes look after the rest. And besides, without toes no one could play "This little piggy went to market"!

Why do feet have arches?

You might think feet could better withstand the pressure of being walked and run on if they were flat instead of arched. But actually the arch is the best shape for supporting weight. Just look at most bridges. To make walking easy, each of your feet has two arches: one that runs from your heel to the ball of your foot to support your weight and one across the ball of your foot to keep you balanced.

Why are feet so ticklish?

If you're like most people, you're probably most ticklish on the soles of your feet. That's because they have a very large concentration of nerve endings, so they're very sensitive. And that's why a tiny stone in your shoe feels like a huge boulder – especially when you walk on it with all your weight.

Why are most people right-handed?

No one really knows for sure, but it was once thought that it was an advantage for ancient warriors to be right-handed. Why? A right-handed warrior would hold his spear in his right hand, leaving his left hand free to hold his shield over the left side of his body and thus protect his heart. Today scientists have thrown out this theory. They now know that handedness is decided in the brain, but they still haven't solved the mystery of why nine out of ten people are right-handers.

Are people left-footed too?

If you're left-handed you're probably left-footed too. And if you're right-handed you probably favor your right foot.

Here's a quick test to find out.

Which foot do you use to kick a ball?
Right ☐   Left ☐

Take off your shoes and socks and pick up a pencil with your toes. Which do you automatically use?
Right ☐   Left ☐
If you used the same foot for both things, that's the foot you prefer. If you had two different answers, you may not have a preference. Does this make you ambipedrous?

Are we born right- or left- handed?

Babies seem to use both hands, but they do have a favorite side. And scientists have found that the hand on the favorite side usually ends up being the preferred hand. To predict which hand a baby will favor when she grows up, watch which side she usually faces when lying on her back. If it's to the right, the baby will probably be right-handed and vice versa.

Can some people use both hands?

Yes. A few people are ambidextrous. That means they can use either hand to do the same task. But that's very rare. Other people are mixed-handed – they can do different tasks with different hands.

Are lefties better at doing certain things?

Some people (probably lefties) claim that left-handed people are more creative and also may do better at subjects requiring logic, such as mathematics. What scientists know for sure is that lefties are better baseball hitters than righties. Scientists think that's because even though left-handers favor their left, they're pretty good with their right too. So they have two good hands on the bat.

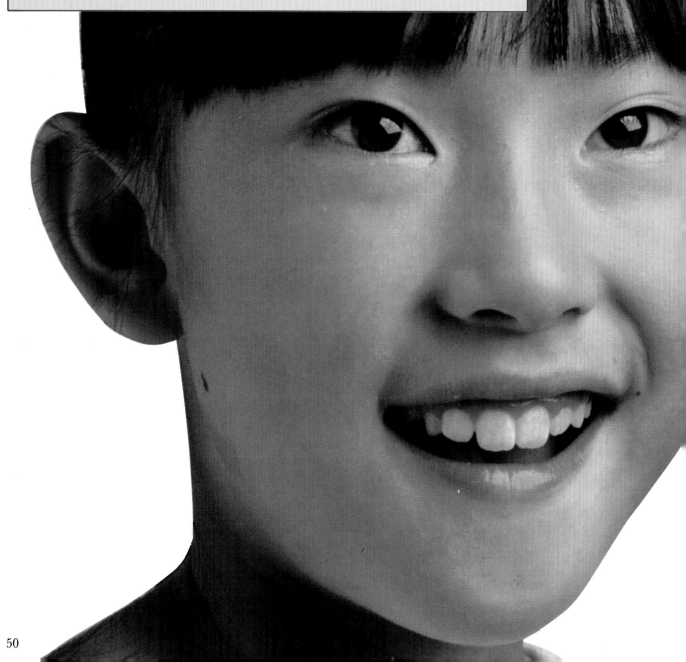

Why do I have a groove connecting my top lip and my nose? ▼

You might not believe this, but that groove is part of a double seam where three pieces of your face joined together. It happened while you were a developing baby inside your mom, and it's visible proof that all your muscles and other soft tissue started growing from your backbone and joined together at your front. On your head, three pieces of facial tissue – two big ones from your cheeks and a smaller one from your nose – met at the center of your top lip. When they fused, the build-up of tissue formed a double seam with a little groove in between. The groove is called the "philtrum." Check out other people's philtra – they come in all shapes and sizes. Just don't stare too long – it's rude!

What causes a "stitch" in your side?

Doctors think the sharp pain you call a stitch sometimes comes when gas builds up after you eat too much. Or it might be caused by a sore diaphragm. This large muscle pushes air in and out of your lungs. The faster you run, the harder it works. When your diaphragm tires, it begins to hurt. That's when you feel a stitch in your side.

Why do my ears pop when I go up in a fast elevator?

That popping sound you hear is your eardrums snapping back after they've bulged out of place. But why do they bulge? When you go up in a really fast elevator, the air pressure outside your ears drops quickly. But the pressure inside your ears doesn't change as fast, resulting in uneven pressure on your eardrums. Groan! To even up the pressure, try swallowing. This opens up the small tube that connects the back of your mouth to the inside of your ears and reduces the pressure by releasing trapped air. Pop!

What's the most powerful muscle in the human body?

YAK YAK YAK

Believe it or not, the most powerful muscle you possess is attached to your head. No, it's not your tongue – it's your jaw muscle. This may surprise you, but it shouldn't. Muscles get stronger by being used. And your jaw muscle gets a lot of exercise.

How can you keep your brain from getting rusty?

In some ways brains are like cars. Some are like Ferraris — they are very sophisticated and can go very fast. Others are more like Volkswagens — slow but sure. But no matter what kind of car (or brain) you have, if you keep it well-oiled you'll get the maximum mileage out of it. And you won't have to worry about "rust."

How you "oil" your brain depends on you. Some people keep their brains from rusting by doing math, others by reading.

What's important is to keep doing whatever it is you're interested in. Why? Your brain is a very complex circuit that runs on electrical impulses. The more inter-connections between the brain's cells, the better the

circuit works. Scientists think that by practicing a task over and over again you help your brain to create new connections that are specifically made for that task. So instead of having to take a long, circuitous route

through your brain, the impulse travels along a short and specific path. The more you practice, the better and faster you'll be.

Help stop your brain from getting rusty by trying this quiz.

Body Quiz

You scratch it, feed it, sleep in it and take it to school. But how much do you really know about your body?

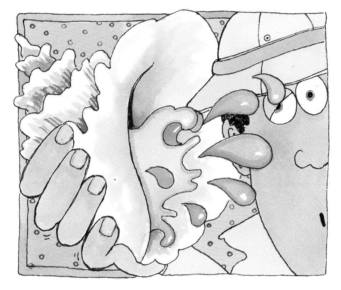

[1] The largest organ in your body is your:
a) brain
b) big toe
c) skin

[2] The air you expel in a sneeze travels about as fast as:
a) a cheetah
b) a hurricane-force wind
c) the speed of sound

[3] If all the blood vessels in your body were laid end to end, they'd stretch:
a) from Toronto to New York
b) across the Atlantic Ocean
c) around the world

[4] Your body contains the same amount of iron as:
a) a steam iron
b) an iron frying pan
c) a small iron nail

[5] The time of day when you're the tallest is:
a) before breakfast
b) at lunch time
c) after dinner

[6] The sound you hear when you put a seashell to your ear is:
a) waves breaking on Waikiki Beach
b) a secret message from a shrimp
c) the echo of blood moving in your ear

[7] During your lifetime you'll likely eat the equivalent weight of:
a) 3 elephants
b) 6 elephants
c) 12 elephants

[8] Your heart is about the same size as your:
a) eyeball
b) fist
c) head

[9] The hardest substance in your body is found in your:
a) thigh bone
b) spine
c) teeth

[10] If your skin could be stretched flat it would cover about the same area as a:
a) postage stamp
b) towel
c) billiard table

[11] When you blush, another part of your body that turns red is:
a) the lining of your stomach
b) your hair
c) your anklebone

[12] Your brain is mostly made of:
a) muscle
b) water
c) mysterious matter from outer space

[13] If all the nerves in your body were placed end to end they'd stretch:
a) from Toronto to New York
b) across the Atlantic Ocean
c) around the world

Check your answers and give yourself one point for each correct answer. Then find out how you rate as a body brain.

■ 0-5: You do have a body, don't you?

■ 6-10: You're nobody's fool!

■ 11-13: You're really a some-body!

Answers:
1. c; 2. b; 3. b; 4. c; 5. a;
6. c; 7. b; 8. b; 9. c; 10. c;
11. a; 12. b; 13. b.

How is it possible to skip a flat rock over water?

It all has to do with bouncing bellyflops. When you bellyflop, you hit the water with your flat front. Ouch! It hurts because for a split second the water resists moving out of your way. You sink immediately, of course, because you're heavy and were travelling downward to begin with. But a flat rock, moving at high speed across the water, does a bouncing bellyflop. Because it only touches the surface for a fraction of a second, the water doesn't have time to get out of the way and let the rock sink. Eventually, the rock slows down, gravity takes over and . . . plop. Time to look for a new rock.

Why can't you see your reflection in rough water?

Look down into choppy water and there's no reflection, right? Wrong. You might not believe this but even when water is rough it's still reflecting. Instead of one smooth surface that looks and acts like a large mirror, however, the waves in rough water make lots of small surfaces that reflect in many different directions. So you get lots of tiny reflections that are so scattered you can't possibly see them all. This doesn't just apply to water. Any surface will reflect, but if it's not smooth the reflection is broken up and unclear.

What makes ice cubes crack when you put them in a drink?

No matter how cold your drink is, it's still warmer than a frozen ice cube. So when you plop in an ice cube, the drink warms up the outside of the cube.

Meanwhile, the inside of the cube stays just as cold as it ever was. Alas, a warm outside that's trying to expand and a cold inside that wants to stay the same means trouble. Eventually the stress becomes too great and – crrrack! Ice cube breakdown.

▲ Why doesn't Earth have a ring around it?

Scientists think that the planets that have rings hold the clue to tell us why Earth *doesn't* have one. The ringed planets, Saturn, Jupiter, Uranus and most probably Neptune, are all giant gas planets, many times bigger and with stronger gravitational forces than Earth. It's easy for them to attract and hold on to chunks of ice, rocks, dust or frozen gas that make up their ring systems. They all have several small moons, which might also help to keep the rings in place. As well, all the gas planets are a great distance from the sun, so their rings aren't exposed to much damage from the powerful solar wind. Compared to these great ringed giants, tiny Earth with its weak gravity, single large moon and closeness to the sun probably never stood much of a chance of holding on to a ring for very long – if at all.

If the earth is moving around the sun, why can't we feel it?

Not only is the earth spinning like a top but it's also moving through space at 250 km/s/155 miles per second. That's a breath-taking speed, so why can't you feel any of this movement? Being on the earth is like being in a smooth elevator. The only way you know it's moving is if it slows down or speeds up. Since the earth travels smoothly at the same speed all the time, there are no changes to let you know you're moving.

Why is the sun yellow?

Next time you barbecue hamburgers, watch the charcoal embers as they cool. They'll turn from white to orange to red. It's the same with stars. The hottest ones burn blue, the coolest red. In between are white, yellow and orange stars. Fortunately for us, our sun is a stable, medium-temperature, yellow star. In late fall, winter and early spring you can see another bright yellow star.

During those times look overhead in the dark night sky for Capella, in the constellation Auriga.

Which is colder, the North or South Pole?

Brrrr. In August 1960 the temperature near the South Pole dropped to a record-breaking -88.3°C/-127°F. The South Pole is usually colder than the North. Why? It's on solid ground, high up on a mountain, where the temperature is colder than at sea level. The North Pole, of course, sits on an ice cap over the Arctic Ocean. You might not think the Arctic Ocean is too warm, but it's warm enough to raise the temperature around the North Pole by a few degrees.

What makes popcorn ◀pop?

Inside every popcorn kernel is a drop or two of water. When you cook corn in very hot oil, the water inside the kernels heats up and begins to turn to steam. As you continue cooking the corn, more and more water becomes steam. Fortunately for popcorn lovers, steam takes up more room than water. So when the steam pressure inside the kernels finally becomes too much for their walls, the popcorn kernels explode – snap, crackle, boom!

How do rubber bands stretch?

If you've ever stretched out a Slinky toy, then let it coil up again, you've seen more or less what happens to the molecules inside a rubber band. Rubber molecules are hooked together so they can stretch into long chains when pulled, then coil up again when the pressure's removed.

Why does a compass always point north?

Did you know that you're whirling through space on a magnet? Yes, the earth is a powerful magnet. A compass needle is also a magnet, though a very tiny one. The north-seeking pole of the compass needle can't help but be attracted to the north pole of the earth.

Why do pennies stink after being in your hand?

Hold a penny tightly in your hand for a few minutes, then sniff it. Yuck! What a stink! There are two things that make that smell – the copper in the penny and your sweat. Copper is a very absorbent metal and it easily picks up sulphur from the air. This not only makes the penny dirty; it also combines with the acids in your perspiration to make hydrogen sulphide. That's the stuff that smells like rotten eggs. The more sulphur and sweat the penny reacts with, the smellier it gets. But remember, it's not worth more just because it's got an extra scent. (Groan!)

Why can't I blow bubbles with regular gum?

All gums contain the same ingredients: flavoring, sweeteners, gum base and wood resin. Yum yum. The flavoring and sweeteners are what make you loyal to your favorite brand, and the gum base is a kind of rubber that keeps your gum from breaking down as you chew it. It's the wood resin, a sticky, elastic substance, that makes chewing gum stretchy. To turn chewing gum into bubble gum, all you need to do is stir in more wood resin. Then when you blow a bubble, the extra wood resin allows the bubble's thin film to keep stretching while you blow and blow until . . .POP! Ooops, better wipe the gum off your face and start again! Even resin has a breaking point.

How ▶ do you make a laser?

LASER is short for "Light Amplification by Stimulated Emission of Radiation." Lasers can be made from gases, liquids or solids, and their power depends on which of these is chosen and how much energy is used to produce them.

A gas laser, for instance, is made by bombarding gas inside a tube with electricity or intense light. This excites the trapped gas, which keeps on building up energy until it must get rid of some of it. As all the tiny, excited bits of gas collide inside the tube, the energy they get rid of creates an incredibly powerful light – laser light.

Will a laser harm you if you get in its way?

Some types of lasers are so powerful they can "zap" you out of your socks.

You certainly wouldn't want to cross the path of the carbon dioxide laser that slices up steel girders or drills holes through diamonds! But low-powered lasers, such as the helium-neon laser that reads the bar codes on your food at check-out counters, won't harm you at all.

Laser light shows are created by argon or krypton gas lasers. When these lasers are shone through glass prisms, they split into the different colors of the rainbow. Though the light from laser shows wouldn't hurt your hand, it could harm your eyes if it shone directly into them. That's why safety barriers are always erected around the laser source at light shows.

Believe it or not, a laser can be focused so precisely that it could be used to put 200 separate holes in the head of a pin!

Why is a laser more powerful than other light beams?

Switch on a flashlight and you'll see that its beam spreads out in a wide V once it leaves the light bulb. But a laser beam doesn't spread out at all. That means that there's no wasted energy, since it's all concentrated in the same direction.

Did You Know That...

• lasers drill holes in baby bottle nipples?
• laser beams carry telephone calls through optical fibers?
• lasers play audio and video discs?
• lasers perform delicate brain, eye and ear surgery?

• industrial lasers weld metals together?
• a laser prints and reads the bar code on your groceries?
• a laser scanner made the color film for this book?

How do fireworks work? ▲

Fireworks are made up of gunpowder and various chemicals. These are all packed into a laminated paper tube along with a small fuse.

Getting a firecracker to burn is a two-stage process. When the fuse is lit the gunpowder explodes, launching the firecracker into the air like a rocket. Once the firecracker is airborne, the fuse ignites the rest of the ingredients. The colors you see showering the sky depend upon the chemicals and metals in the firecracker. Different chemicals burn in different colors. Strontium and lithium compounds, for example, burn red, barium ones burn green, copper salts and compounds burn blue, and sodium ones burn yellow. Carbon and metallic lead, iron and aluminum create sparks, and charcoal is sometimes used to create the brightly colored "tails" that streak across the dark night sky.

All these chemicals mean that fireworks displays are very dangerous. So make sure you get an expert to set off your next show.

How can you make glow-in-the-dark stuff?

Take a few Wintergreen Life Savers and a mirror into a *very* dark closet. Pop two candies into your mouth and, watching your open mouth in the mirror, crunch down on them. If you crunch hard enough you should see a green flash. Why? Scientists think they've finally found the answer for this phenomenon, which is called "triboluminescence." They've discovered that the flashes come from the way the crystals in certain materials are put together. The crystals of triboluminescent material are arranged irregularly. So when these crystals break apart, positive and negative electrical charges in the crystals separate, leaving holes between them. The charges then leap across these spaces to recombine. These "leaps" stir up nitrogen molecules in the air and produce a blue-green glow, which is the flash you see.

Why do some Frisbees glow in the dark?

There's nothing quite as magic as a yo-yo or a Frisbee glowing in the dark. How do they do it? They glow because they're made of special phosphorescent compounds.

Any object absorbs energy when light is shone on it. The light "excites" the molecules within the object, making them highly energized.

However, these molecules would prefer to return to the calm, relaxed state they were in before the light started shining. To release their excess energy and get back to normal, they radiate the energy in the form of light and heat. Usually the light is radiated much too quickly for the human eye to see. But with some special compounds, such as calcium sulphide, the light trickles out over seconds or hours. And it's that stored-up light you see glowing in the dark as it's released.

How many stars are there in the Milky Way Galaxy? ▼

Our home galaxy, the Milky Way, is a city of stars – perhaps as many as 200 billion of them. The sun is merely one star among all those billions. The Milky Way is a spiral galaxy, shaped a bit like a Frisbee. Earth is inside the "Frisbee," about halfway between one edge and the middle. That's one reason why every star you can see from Earth belongs to our galaxy. How many can you see? If you're stargazing in the city, you'll be lucky if you can see 200. Away from lights, however, you might see as many as 4,000.

Can you ever see rainbows at night?

Rainbows *do* happen at night, although they are usually much harder to see than those that color the daytime sky. Next time you see bright moonlight shining down upon falling water, look closely. You may be able to spot faint nighttime rainbows. Two huge African waterfalls are famous for their mysterious moonbows. Moonbows? They're like rainbows, only they're made from moonbeams, not sunbeams.

Why do stars twinkle?

It's because they're so far away. Our nearest star after the sun is so distant that its light reaches Earth as a tiny pinpoint. Any movement of air in our atmosphere causes this pinpoint of light to waver, or twinkle. You can use this fact to decide if you're watching a star or planet, because planets don't twinkle. The light from a planet reaches Earth as a much bigger bundle of light because it's close enough to be seen as a disc, not merely a pinpoint. The larger the bundle of light, therefore, that reaches Earth, the less it's affected by our turbulent atmosphere and the more constant it appears to us. Besides, "Twinkle, twinkle little planet" just doesn't sound right!

Is there such a thing as stardust?

Yes. When a star explodes, pieces of the star blast out into space. Some of this "stardust" is as small as earth dust; some of it is the size of boulders. The stardust floats around until it's sucked into another star or enough of it gathers together to form a new planet. Scientists believe that Earth might have been formed when flecks and chunks of stardust swirled together into a ball. If you'd like to see some stardust for yourself, look under your bed. Chances are there's some stardust in among the other bits of dust you'll find there, because Earth still picks up more than 1,000 tons of stardust a day as it travels through space.

How do bats fly?

It takes you approximately a second to say the word "bat." In this short time, a bat can flap its wings 10 times. No wonder you can't see it clearly.

Scott Altenbach's extraordinary stop-motion photographs reveal how the world's only flying mammal stays aloft and exactly how it flaps its wings to fly. These photographs of the fringe-lipped bat stop motion at one ten-thousandth of a second.

1 The start of a downstroke. This begins the movement of air that lifts the bat's body upwards.

2 The wings, continuing downwards, start to swivel forward.

3 Just before the downstroke is completed, the bat's body gets the maximum amount of lift to send it through the air.

4 Now the wings are about to begin an upstroke.

5 When the wings are folded in, there is little drag through the air.

6 Next is the start of an upward flick, which gives the bat's body even more lift.

7 When the flick is finished, the bat is ready to begin another downstroke.

8 The wing beat starts again.

Why can't I float in my bathtub?

Dive into a pool and you soon bob up to the surface. But climb into a bathtub and you remain sitting on the bottom. Why do you float in a big pool and sink in a small tub? The size of the container and the amount of water in it makes the difference. To float, there must be enough water for you to sink down to the point of "equilibrium." What's equilibrium? It's the point at which your body pushes out of the way an amount of water that weighs the same as you – the rest of the liquid, which had been holding up that water, holds you up instead. In a big pool there's room for you to push the water out of the way and still have plenty of water left between you and the bottom of the pool. Because your weight equals the weight of the water you've moved, you float. But in a bathtub, unless it happens to be huge and you're very small, you weigh more than the water you're able to move, so you sink.

How did people figure out soap would get you clean?

Until about 2,000 years ago people in Europe washed by coating themselves with mud, then scraping it off with an iron instrument. To soothe their sore skin, they rubbed oil all over themselves. In those days, oily skin was considered beautiful. It was the Gauls from Southern France who invented soap. They used to plaster their hair with goat fat and ash to make it fashionably stiff. They then discovered that when they mixed their hair "gel" with water, it cleaned dirt and grease off their skin. Now oily skin isn't too trendy – except at the beach.

What are bathtubs made of?

The first modern bathtubs were wooden. Some were plated with metal, but they were scratchy and leaked. Rich people bought smooth china bathtubs, but they were so cold you had to put pillows inside to sit on. Then all-metal baths arrived – they were smooth and warmed up quickly. These tubs were covered in paint to keep them from rusting. But the paint sometimes dissolved in hot water, turning the unlucky bather a peculiar color. Finally, someone decided to cover a metal tub in hard enamel. At last, a truly comfortable bath. The quest for the best bathtub continues, however. The latest tubs are made of acrylic. Their main advantage? They aren't cold when you lean back for a soak and a good read.

How did people clean their teeth before toothbrushes were invented?

The first toothbrush was a good-tasting twig, chewed until one end shredded and could be used as a brush.

In many places people still chew a stick a day. Later, hardy types cleaned their teeth with a finger dipped in salt or chalk. Toothpicks were popular – the rich wore jeweled picks on chains or stuck them in their hats. Toothbrushes with gold and silver handles and hog bristles arrived 300 years ago. Wooden ones cheap enough for most people to buy arrived 200 years later. And the rest is history.

How much water do you use in a day?

If you're like the average North American, you use about 325 L/71 gal – more than two bathtubs full. But what do you do with all that water? For instance, how much water do you flush down the toilet every day?

Check out these figures: flushing the toilet uses up 110 L/22 gal, watering the garden, washing the car, 90 L/20 gal, drinking and cooking, 11 L/2 gal, washing clothes, dishes and self, 124 L/27 gal.

(P.S. If you gave up having baths, washing dishes and doing laundry, you could cut your family's water bill by almost a third.)

Why do you get sleepy at the end of the day?

Your reliable, light-sensitive internal alarm clock keeps you on schedule and tells you it's time to go to sleep. Happy dreams.

Why do my eyelids weigh so much when I'm tired?

Your eyelids don't really get heavier when you're tired, it's just that you lose control over them. When you're asleep, your whole body begins to relax. Instead of being ready for action, your muscles go limp and won't do what you want them to. You're absolutely right when you say "I'm so tired I can't keep my eyes open." And haven't you noticed at about the time your eyelids start to droop, how your arms and legs feel oh so heavy, your head nods forward and next thing you know . .

What happens to my body when I fall asleep?

Sleep is like a mini-holiday for your brain and body: everything relaxes. And because relaxed muscles need less oxygen, your breathing and heart beat slow down. Once this happens, you start to sweat and your body temperature drops slightly. Then about an hour after you fall asleep, your eyeballs start moving rapidly beneath your eyelids as you begin to dream. You drift in and out of dream sleep all night until – rrring! – your alarm clock tells your body the holiday is over.

How often do we dream?

People dream four or five times a night, each dream lasting longer than the one before. Most of us spend as much as two hours a night dreaming.

To tell if someone's dreaming, watch him closely while he sleeps. If he's lying very still and his eyeballs are moving rapidly beneath his eyelids, he's dreaming. Are his eyes watching what's happening in his dream? No one knows.

What happens to your brain and your body during dreams?

Your brain works by electricity. If this electricity were visible, your brain would appear to be glowing brightly when you are awake. But your sleeping brain would have only an odd spark here and there, except during dreams. Then your brain would glow as if it were awake!

You can toss and turn most of the night, but never while dreaming. That's because your muscles go limp during dreams. Perhaps your brain prevents your muscles from moving so that you don't hurt yourself.

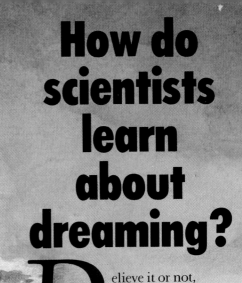

How do scientists learn about dreaming?

Believe it or not, there are places called sleep labs, and people stay overnight there. While they're sleeping, scientists record their brain electricity. It's possible to tell from a brain's electrical activity when a dream starts and ends, but not what the dream was about.

What do animals dream about?

Reptiles and amphibians probably don't dream at all, but it seems that most warm-blooded animals do. All, that is, except for the spiny anteater. Scientists have discovered that this mammal never dreams, but they don't know why.

Cats that have been operated on so that their muscles don't go limp during dreams, have been seen running while asleep, and sometimes even attacking imaginary mice.

Do babies dream?

Newborn babies are great dreamers: they spend about half their sleep time dreaming. Babies even dream before they're born! What do you suppose an unborn baby dreams about?

Why is the moon round?

If you think the moon is round, guess again. It's egg-shaped, and the pointed end, which has the thinner crust, always faces the earth.

Some scientists think that the earth's strong gravitational pull may have sucked the moon into this shape.

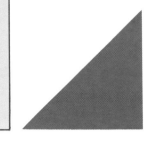

Where did the moon come from?

Even though the moon is Earth's nearest neighbor in space, astronomers still aren't sure how it formed. The best theory is that another planet about the size of Mars smashed into Earth just after it formed. When the crash happened, a huge amount of rock was blasted off into the space around Earth. Later, this material collected into a body one-quarter the size of the earth's diameter – and became known as the moon.

Could a balloon float up to the moon?

Think of how much money NASA would save if astronauts could travel to the moon by balloon! Alas, it will never happen. To rise, balloons must be filled with a gas that's lighter than air. But if they rise high enough above the earth, the air they're floating through becomes as thin and "light" as the gas inside the balloon. And once the balloon isn't lighter than the air, it will stop rising. Scientists think a balloon could rise about 30 km/20 miles before it stopped dead. So much for ballooning to the moon.

Is there ever a blue moon?

Once in a blue moon, the moon really does appear to turn blue. The last time a blue moon was seen was in 1950. Scientists believe it was caused when a thicker than usual blanket of dust filtered out red light in the earth's atmosphere, leaving the moon looking decidedly blue.

Can you ever see the other side of the moon?

You won't ever see this view of the moon from your bedroom window. It's the far side of the moon and it's never visible from Earth. The moon is locked so tightly into its orbit by the earth's strong gravitational pull that it can't turn fast enough to show us its other side.

INDEX

PHOTO and ILLUSTRATION CREDITS

pp. 8-9 Terry Shoffner;
10-11 Tony Thomas;
12-13 Tony Thomas, Tina Holdcroft;
14-15 Tony Thomas;
16 M. Thonig/ H. Armstrong Roberts/Miller Services Limited;
18-19 Nigel Dickson;
20-21 Tony Thomas, Tina Holdcroft;
22 Patti Murray/Animals Animals;
23 Animals Animals/

Oxford Scientific Films, Jonathan Coddington, Dr. T. Eisner;
24-25 Greg McEvoy (Tyler*Clark);
26-27 Adrienne Gibson/ Animals Animals;
28 Bruno Kern;
29 Tina Holdcroft;
30-31 Ray Boudreau, Tina Holdcroft;
32 Tony Thomas;
33 Tina Holdcroft;
34 Tony Thomas;

35 Tina Holdcroft;
36-37 Tony Thomas;
38-39 Tony Thomas;
40-41 Tony Thomas;
42-43 Tony Thomas;
44-45 Shun Sasabuchi;
46-47 Tony Thomas;
48-49 Tony Thomas; Tina Holdcroft;
50 Tony Thomas;
51 Tina Holdcroft;
52-53 Nigel Dickson, Tina Holdcroft;
54-55 Ray Boudreau;
56 David Edmonds;

57 Tina Holdcroft;
58-59 Tony Thomas;
60-61 © Robert Isear/Science Source;
62 Tony Thomas;
63 Tina Holdcroft;
64-65 Tony Thomas;
66-67 Scott Altenbach;
68-69 Tony Thomas;
70 Tony Thomas;
71 Tina Holdcroft;
72-73 Maryanne Kovalski;
75 NASA

Front Cover: Tony Thomas

CONSULTANTS

Dr. R. Anderson;
Dr. D.B. Bonder, *Humber Equine Clinic;*
Dr. David Carr, *McMaster University Medical Centre;*
Dr. D. Chute, *Department of Life Sciences, University of Toronto;*
Dr. B. Colman, *Department of Biology, York University;*
D. H. Cormack, *Department of Anatomy, University of Toronto;*
Dr. I. G. Currie, *Department of Mechanical Engineering, University of Toronto;*
Terry Dickinson, *Astronomy Specialist;*
Dr. G. Drake;
Dr. James Eckenwalder, *Department of Botany, University of Toronto;*

Dr. D. Ellis, *Department of Otolaryngology, University of Toronto;*
Dr. J. Grayson, *Department of Physiology, Faculty of Medicine, University of Toronto;*
Arthur Grosser;
Dr. B.R. Krafchik, *Associate Professor, Faculty of Medicine, University of Toronto;*
Ross James, *Department of Ornithology, Royal Ontario Museum;*
Dr. Gary Landsberg, *Thornhill, Ontario;*
Dr. P.J. Lea, *Department of Anatomy, University of Toronto;*
Professor George Lewis, *McMaster University Medical Centre;*

Jim Lovisek, *Toronto Nature Centre;*
Ross MacCulloch, *Department of Ichthyology and Herpetology, Royal Ontario Museum;*
Elizabeth MacLeod, *Managing Editor, OWL Magazine;*
Bob McDonald, *science writer and broadcaster;*
Dr. Hooley McLaughlin, *Ontario Science Centre;*
Paul McManus;
Dr. K.G. McNeill, *Department of Physics, University of Toronto;*
Dr. Betty Roots, *Chairman, Department of Zoology, University of Toronto;*

Dr. R. Schemenauer, *Environment Canada;*
Dr. M. Schlesinger;
Dr. Thomas Swatland, *Department of Animal and Poultry Science, University of Guelph;*
Dr. M. Taylor, *D.V.M., Martin Veterinary Hospital;*
Dr. J.M. Toguri, *Department of Metallurgy and Materials Science, University of Toronto;*
Dr. Stephen Wallace, *Department of Chemistry, University of Toronto;*
Susan Woodward, *Department of Mammalogy, Royal Ontario Museum.*